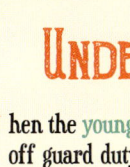

Under Wraps

When the young private turned on the light in the showers after coming off guard duty early in the morning, he could hardly miss the large sack standing in the middle of the room. It was made of fine blue cloth and tied with a gaudy ribbon. Either Father Christmas had lost a sack of presents or else someone was having a laugh at the men's expense.

The soldier hurried to wake up his comrades and together they tried to undo the ribbon, which wasn't as easy as it looked. When they finally managed to open the sack, there were no presents waiting for them. Instead, they found their comrade Private Jim Honington – as dead as a doornail. His face was blue and his limbs were already stiff, but he looked very peaceful lying there. There was no sign of a fight, though a strong smell of alcohol exuded from the body.

The officer on duty notified the police at once. When Inspector Lestrade arrived accompanied by his assistants, he sent for Holmes immediately. "This kind of tomfoolery doesn't suit a rational mind like mine," he said to Holmes when he arrived at the crime scene. "This is your department."

The master detective took a quick look at the dead man as he ran a hand over the sack and wound the ribbon through his fingers. "Which battalion is this?" he asked the officer.

"The Tenth Paratroopers, sir!"

"Well then, get the men to line up."

"For questioning as witnesses? Or do you think one of my boys did this?"

"I'm afraid I do."

"Just the man for the job," Lestrade said, sounding rather pleased with himself. "Let's see Father Christmas wriggle his way out of this one."

(Turn Page for Solution)

AF133331

UNDER WRAPS   Solution

As soon as all the soldiers had lined up in front of the sack containing the dead man, the detective looked them over one by one with piercing eyes. Eventually he addressed them all. "Jim Honington wasn't what you would call popular, was he?"

When the soldiers failed to reply, the officer spoke up for them: "He was a bit of a miser as far as the men were concerned."

"Methinks someone wanted to teach the scrooge of the airborne forces a lesson in time for Christmas, and the young men hatched out a plan. They made a sack large enough to hold someone his size and after lights out, they hauled said scrooge out of bed for a round of drinks. Nothing out of the ordinary for a bunch of young soldiers – Honington reeks of alcohol even now. They got him so drunk that he could no longer defend for himself and then they popped him into the sack, which is why there are no signs of a fight. Then they tied up the sack and left him to mull over his miserly ways, evoking that scary Christmas tale where Saint Nick sticks all the naughty children in his sack. Unfortunately, the material used for the sack was parachute silk, probably because it is so strong. In the military, parachute silk is always blue to make it invisible against the sky. More importantly in this case, however, it is also almost airtight to ensure the necessary air resistance for a safe descent!"

One of the soldiers started to snivel but Holmes continued.

"Tied up in his sack, the soldier was put somewhere where no one would find him until the next day. I'm afraid it wasn't long before he ran out of air. Young Honington suffocated."

"Jim was always happy to drink so long as he didn't have to pay, but he'd never offer to get the next round." The sniveling soldier said.

"It was an accident!" said a second soldier, stepping forward.

"No, it was reckless stupidity which cost your comrade his life." Holmes corrected him. "And will probably put the two of you behind bars."

A Coded Affair

Mr Holmes, I require your services to catch my unfaithful spouse!" the stranger said as he shook a large amount of snow off his overcoat onto Mr Holmes' doormat.

"It's beneath my dignity to squander my skills on squabbling couples I'm afraid."

Dr Watson, sitting beside the fire, turned away to hide the grin he was unable to stifle. The tall visitor stopped in surprise. Then he raised his eyebrows sarcastically. "Beneath your dignity, well I never. No doubt, this worrisome coded message would prove too difficult for you to solve. I found it on my wife's bedside table. She is a perfidious creature, I can tell you, who associates with the worst kind of men. The fact that it is written in code clearly demonstrates her base nature."

"A coded message?" Holmes inquired. "Oh all right, I'll take a look. I'll solve it faster than it takes to tell you I am not interested in your profane problems." The man hesitated for a moment as he swallowed his pride but then he handed Holmes a folded note. "This is the message. It must surely be from her lover. Unfortunately, I have not been able to solve it."

Mr Holmes glanced at the piece of paper and said almost immediately: "I shall read you the message but I demand you leave my house the moment I have finished."

Dear Mrs Fraud,

```
Y B H O T I F T S O H
O A E N H K R H T T S
U N A Y R E I A F H T
R D T O O E D L I E R
H I I U S A A F V H E
U S N W E C Y P E I E
S C G I P H A A 5 G T
```

A friend

A Coded Affair

"Are you familiar with Chinese script?" Holmes asked. The tall man stared at him in alarm: "Is she betraying me with a Chinese man?" Dr Watson watched his friend roll his eyes impatiently: "It says nothing about that here. Neither if nor with whom your wife might be betraying you."

"But the note is for my wife – from a friend, it says!"

Ignoring this interjection, Holmes continued: "You have to look at each row separately, moving from top to bottom and from left to right. Like ancient Chinese writing. It is a tried and tested form of code even though it is very simple. It reads thus:

Dear Mrs Fraud,

YOUR HUSBAND IS CHEATING ON YOU WITH ROSE PIKE EACH FRIDAY AT HALF PAST FIVE 50 THE HIGH STREET

A friend"

The man turned white and looked at Holmes indignantly, as if he were to blame for his troubles. "Mr Fraud – I assume that's your name – I would appreciate it if you would spare me the details. If you continue to drench my doormat for much longer, I will charge you my usual fee."

Before Holmes could finish what he was saying, the man turned on the spot. Without another word, he disappeared into the blizzard raging outside in London's empty streets.

PRESENT AND CORRECT

F ollowing the case at Wisteria Lodge, Mr Holmes received an official thank-you letter from San Pedro in South America and a special accolade from Spain: An invitation to the Christmas reception at the Spanish Consulate in Belgravia Square. Many dignitaries including the Earl of Sandwich were expected to attend. At the annual Diplomats' Conference, the Earl had come to blows with Spain's previous chief diplomat on the issue of how to make a good sandwich. Subsequently he had persuaded the government to have the man removed from his post. Relations between the two countries had cooled considerably since then and it was hoped the Christmas reception would placate feelings all round.

Christmas receptions were not exactly Mr Holmes' cup of tea. He absent-mindedly accepted compliments about his last case, refused to engage in conversation and spent most of his time trying to determine from which part of London people had travelled by studying the specks of dirt on their clothing.

At the climax of the festivities, Chief Spanish Diplomat Martí Deulofeu, who had only taken over the post a few months previously, stepped forward and addressed the Earl: "We are greatly honoured to welcome you here tonight. As a small token of our affection, please allow me to present you with a traditional nativity scene from my home of Catalonia – in the hope that it will find a prime position at Mapperton House."

As the guests applauded, several servants carried a nativity crib covered in silk into the room and set it down in front of the Earl. When he lifted the cloth and cautiously peered underneath, his eyes widened in astonishment. A murmur of disbelief ran through the room. The figure of a man in coarse clothing was set next to Mary, Joseph and the baby Jesus in the stable. With his trousers down and an insolent stare on his face, he was in the process of defecating.

"How dare you!" the insulted Earl exclaimed.

Mr Holmes let out a hearty laugh, breaking the shocked silence.

PRESENT AND CORRECT Solution

"My dear Earl, don't be offended - El Caganer is not intended as an insult; in fact, the figurine is part of the Catalan nativity tradition. The defecating figure dressed in a traditional Catalan costume is often found near the stable.

Señor Deulofeu will no doubt agree that there are many plausible and as many implausible reasons for this regional oddity. No one knows what the Caganer is really meant to symbolise. The Catholic Church accepts it as a part of the nativity scene, however, and similar figures exist in France, Portugal or even the city of Naples. I believe there is also a German equivalent called the Cholera Man.

I hope you have learnt a little more about the customs of the Catalans this evening. I am sure Senor Deulofeu now understands that not everyone in England is familiar with Catalan Christmas traditions. 'Menja bé, caga fort i no tinguis por a la mort!' as the Catalans say, though I'd rather not translate that if you don't mind, for decency's sake."

The Christmas Show in Camden Town

Bernulli was a tightrope artist, Holmes. He died yesterday – at approximately 5.45 pm. He was on his own in the great hall at the variety theatre next to Camden Stables, practising for this year's Christmas show."

"Allow me to guess how he died, dear Lestrade!"

"Go on then, Holmes!"

"He fell from the wire!"

"He did indeed, although he was an absolute professional. That is why he never worked with a safety harness – it was his downfall in the end. The wire was suspended more than thirty feet above the ground, Holmes! And here's a strange thing: We found this note in his left trouser pocket."

WATCH OUT! SALVATORE WANTS YOU OUT OF THE WAY! TODAY! DECEMBER 3RD. K.

"We don't know who K. is yet, but Salvatore is another tightrope walker and Bernulli's greatest rival, although he's nowhere near as good. He wasn't in the hall at the time of the accident though. He was down in the cellar where the dressing rooms are. The stairs are directly opposite the porter's lodge – and there is no other way down! Salvatore and Bernulli arrived at the same time – they were the only ones here last night. Salvatore went to the cellar and Bernulli went to the hall. The porter was at his post next to the stage entrance the whole time. A short time later, the director arrived to see Bernulli and found him dead. We have checked everything: No greased wire. No damaging substances in Bernulli's body. No hidden fireworks. No trace of a clue. It is as if Salvatore pushed Bernulli off the wire using telekinetic powers. He keeps telling us that Bernulli had been drinking a lot lately. We actually did find two open bottles of gin in Bernulli's dressing room in the cellar, but they are both covered in Salvatore's fingerprints. Also, there was no trace of alcohol in Bernulli's blood. So, is Salvatore lying? It must be more than coincidence."

"I agree, Lestrade. It is most peculiar! However, I can see how Salvatore might have killed the tightrope walker Bernulli without leaving the cellar."

THE CHRISTMAS SHOW IN CAMDEN TOWN

"5.45 pm you say, Lestrade? It is pitch black at that time of the evening, is it not? So, the two artists arrive at the theatre. The victim heads to the great hall to practise his act on the tightrope. Salvatore goes down to the cellar - apparently on his way to the artists' dressing rooms. I am sure the porter will be able to confirm this course of events precisely. So how did Salvatore manage to murder the tightrope artist in the great hall without leaving the cellar? On first sight, it seems impossible. However, most buildings' fuse boxes are installed in the cellar. Salvatore opens the fuse box, then after the given interval it would take for Bernulli to climb onto the wire, he unplugs the fuse for the electricity supply to the great hall. Suddenly Bernulli is surrounded by total darkness. He cannot see a thing and immediately loses his balance. There is no time for his eyes to adapt to the dark before he falls. A few seconds later Salvatore plugs the fuse back into the box.

Lestrade, that's what must have happened. If the gin bottles are anything to go by, there is a fair chance our culprit was reckless enough not to don gloves. Find the fuse box and the fuse for the great hall, and check it for Salvatore's fingerprints. I am almost certain you will be successful . . ."

The Good and the Bad

A constant flow of batter chugged out of the machine, down stainless steel chutes, and through a filler, into the bowls waiting to be sealed with airtight lids. During the Christmas season, pre-packed Plum Puddings were the big seller. A conveyor belt transferred the finished products to a refrigerated warehouse. There, a worker in thickly lined overalls lay on the ground next to an empty pallet labelled 'scrap'. He was choking desperately. His face had turned a bluish-red.

Dr Watson who had been called to the scene of the accident examined the man. He was almost unconscious and his lips were covered in pudding batter.

"If we have to halt production because of this, it will be the ruin of us!" howled the American factory owner who had summoned Watson and was now standing nervously behind him. "What happened?" asked Watson.

"At Christmas time, it's a back-breaking job working here. Mr Dickins works in the cold store, loading the pallets. He must have been hungry and decided to eat one of the Christmas puddings. Shortly afterwards he collapsed ... Of course, eating on the job is strictly forbidden. Especially from our own stock! I went over immediately, but no one saw what actually happened – he usually works by himself in there." – "Could the mixture be contaminated?" – The owner shook his head. "We just did a routine check a few minutes ago: Everything is fine."

"Are there any hard ingredients in the puddings?"

"Just the obligatory sixpence in about every fifth portion, to bring good luck for the following year to whoever finds it. But it's made of sugar these days and is actually smaller than a real one. You wouldn't choke on that."

Watson forced open the semiconscious man's jaws and peered into his mouth. "Ah!" he said, and hurriedly searched through his doctor's bag. He pulled out a long pair of forceps and plunged them down the man's throat. A huge coin appeared. The worker on the ground gasped, drawing a liberated breath. "This, my good man," said the doctor, holding up the coin, "is not a sixpence; it's an American silver dollar. How it came to be stuck in this man's throat is for the experts to determine. I happen to know someone who fits the bill ..."

The Good and the Bad   Solution

"Practically unconscious, not to mention the colour of his face - the poor man was close to suffocating. The reason, of course, was the silver dollar stuck in the middle of his oesophagus which, because of its size, was blocking his windpipe," Watson explained to his friend as soon as Mr Holmes arrived at the factory. "But how did it get into the mixture?"

"The Americans like to use their dollar coins to tighten screws because they are so robust," said the master detective. He looked sternly at the factory owner: "Am I correct in assuming that this is not the first time the victim tampered with the company's puddings?"

"What makes you think that?"

"You mentioned Mr Dickins worked alone in the cold store, but you were at his side immediately. I suspect that he had been eating Christmas puddings on a regular basis, to keep himself going between meals - and that you had noticed. You spied on him and discovered that he liked to help himself to the rejected items which were taken off the production line and collected on a separate pallet. They are always destroyed, so any missing ones would go unnoticed. You wanted to catch your employee red-handed. Therefore, you placed a plum pudding prepared with a silver dollar instead of the usual sugar sixpence on the said pallet and lay in wait inside the cold store. The employee started to eat the dough, and you jumped out of your hiding place to confront him. The dollar in his mouth was supposed to convict him. But rather than admit anything, Mr Dickins tried to swallow the coin despite its size - whether he underestimated the diameter of it or overestimated the diameter of his oesophagus remains to be seen."

"That's the Christmas Spirit you wouldn't even let him have the duds!" said Watson to the factory owner.

"There are hygienic reasons, amongst other things," the latter defended himself, sounding quite put out.

"If I hadn't turned up so quickly, your mission could easily have ended up being fatal . . ."

"I'll keep the silver dollar, if you don't mind," Holmes said.

"You don't think I'm stupid enough to hide it in another Christmas pud, do you?"

"Of course not, but there's a screw loose on my desk."

Gifts from Saint Nick

"Mr Holmes! Mr Holmes!" Mr Holmes increased his step, but old Mrs Mug was exceedingly quick for her age. "Oh, Mrs Mug, I'm so sorry, I didn't hear you. I'm afraid I must dash. Scotland Yard has just summoned me to the scene of a crime. The night before last, a bank was broken into just around the corner and the Yard is at a loss for what to do next."

"I know all about it, I live right next door. Someone cut open the safe with a blowtorch! But that's not what I wanted to tell you. Let me walk along with you and explain what has happened to me this time!" Holmes gave her a crooked smile. He was familiar with Mrs Mug's stories - she thought a crime was lurking behind every corner, but her tip-offs always turned out to be nothing but paranoia. "This morning my boots and those of all my neighbours were filled with presents. Tangerines, walnuts and even a whole ham for each of us! It is very suspicious, although none of my neighbours have dropped dead yet. So there's no sign of poison at the moment." - "Perhaps someone wanted to give you all a lovely surprise? Or it was a Christmas charity effort." There were many poorer working class families living in Mrs Mug's building. She snorted scornfully. "You know what else is funny? There was nothing left outside the Tott family's door in the basement flat. Two lovely boys, very decent and helpful, live there with their widowed mother. They look after her with such devotion and they always carry my shopping up to the third floor. Maybe the Totts intimidated whoever is trying to poison or blackmail the rest of us. The two of them are built like tanks - you wouldn't argue with them if you could help it. They work on building sites most of the year. This summer they were at the Tower Bridge site while the railings were renewed. It's just in the winter they get laid off." - "You suppose it could be blackmail?" Holmes stopped in his tracks.

"There's no such thing as charity these days. You never get something for nothing. It must be some foul trick or other. We will all find ransom notes in our letterboxes tomorrow, telling us to pay up for anything we've eaten, or else . . . I hope it isn't poison, but I'm not an idiot! I haven't touched a thing."

"Mrs Mug, I believe you just might have helped me solve a crime for the first time in your life, and I haven't even inspected the crime scene yet."

"Lestrade, I think I know who did it," Holmes greeted the police inspector when he arrived at the crime scene. Lestrade raised an eyebrow wearily. "Hold your horses, Holmes, not even you could do that." - "I've just talked to a lady who lives in the house next door. All the residents there received gifts this morning, except for a family with two grown-up sons living in the basement." - "Holmes, would you come with me and take a look at the cut open safes first." - "One moment, Lestrade. The boys are builders. This year they worked on renewing the railings at Tower Bridge. What sort of tools do you need for that kind of work, would you say?"

Lestrade's eyes suddenly flashed with excitement: "Blowtorches." Holmes nodded: "Mrs Mugs just told me the two of them are usually unemployed in the winter months. There is hardly any building work going on at the end of the year. So at Christmas time they run out of money. I am willing to wager they pilfered a blowtorch while they were working on the bridge, then dug a tunnel from their flat to the bank vaults and cut open the safes with the tools they'd stolen."

"You deduce all that from a bit of circumstantial evidence suggesting the two of them bestowed gifts upon their neighbours on Saint Nicholas Day?" - "I'm off to investigate the Tott brothers immediately. I promise you, they are a pair of Robin Hoods for sure."

A Christmas Crash

At first, all they could hear was a humming sound growing continuously louder, and then eventually, they spotted a small plane between the low clouds. "I say, Holmes!" Holmes retorted with an unimpressed-sounding "Pff. It's just an advertisement." He was right. The plane was pulling a banner along behind it, announcing the Christmas bargains at a local department store: 20% off everything when you shout 'knockout prices' at the counter!

"A cheap swizzle if you ask me," Holmes said.

The plane flew in circles over the city leaving a trail of white condensation. All at once, the trail stopped and then the banner suddenly ballooned to four times its size, fluttering large and red in the sky!

By this time, Holmes had come to the window, too, and was staring out in alarm.

"What an amazing show!" Watson exclaimed.

"I'm afraid we're going see a real knockout in a minute."

"What are you talking about?"

Sure enough, a few moments later the plane went into a steep and precarious-looking descent. Again and again, the nose of the plane pulled up and then lurched back down again. It drew a slow final circle just above the rooftops before disappearing out of sight a few streets away from Baker Street and Holmes and Watson's viewpoint.

"Come on Holmes, we must get over there at once. The pilot might be injured!" Watson shouted.

"And the police are bound to destroy the evidence."

"What evidence?"

"Evidence of sabotage of course." Holmes had already put on his coat and shoes while Watson was still busy looking for his doctor's bag. "Didn't you notice?"

A Christmas Crash Solution

There was nothing they could do for the pilot. He had picked a quiet side street for his emergency landing. However, just as he touched down, a lorry loaded with Christmas trees pulled out of an entrance. The plane had crashed into it with full force. Now it was stuck there. The wings had broken off and the tail fin protruded into the air. The pilot's cabin was smashed to bits.

Once Watson had made his way across the trailer of the lorry to the pilot and confirmed that he was dead, he returned to Holmes, who was busy examining the plane-wreck together with several police officers.

"He was as good as dead the moment he took off, he just didn't realise it," the detective said.

One of the police officers asked: "How would he have been able to foresee an accident?"

"This was no accident."

The man pulled out his notebook. "Are you sure, Mr Holmes?"

"For one thing: the emissions from the exhaust. The combustion product of kerosene, or airplane fuel if you prefer, condenses to form white plumes of smoke. When the smoke stopped suddenly, the fuel tank must have been empty – long before the plane was due to land. Fuel must have been dumped secretly in advance. No pilot would ever intentionally begin to glide with a banner attached to the tail of his aircraft – it would slow down the flight speed too much, a bit like using a braking parachute. Of course, the lack of fuel could have been due to some mistake during refuelling, or because of a leak in the fuel tank. The unfolding banner, however, is clearly the work of a saboteur. At that size, the brake effect would be a danger for any aeroplane, even without a stalled engine. The two problems combined were bound to prove fatal. The real advertising banner must have been replaced before takeoff. The one used was made of several folded layers of fabric instead of just the one. The different layers were probably tacked together very loosely. They came undone as the banner faced the headwind and filled with air. I suggest you start your inquiries by looking for any rivals of the department store. Who else has similar goods on offer and could have had access to the advertising banner? Once you find that out, you'll find the perpetrator in no time at all."

A Mole in the Works

A commotion at Scotland Yard! Once again, in just a short space of time, Professor Moriarty had managed to elude a cleverly laid trap. At London police HQs, everyone was certain: an internal leak must be to blame. How else could the master of crime always spot the danger in advance?

"We are going to set another trap," Inspector Lestrade confided to Mr Holmes whom he had invited over to the office for a glass of hot Christmas punch. "And it had better work this time, or else I'll be the laughing stock of the force. To be honest, I'm almost certain I know who our mole is – our new colleague Mrs Browner. She's only been here a couple of months – she joined us just as we began developing our current plans to catch Moriarty. She is not directly involved in the work, but her desk in the open-plan office is right next to the Moriarty task force. I wager she can overhear important information which she then passes on to Moriarty's middlemen. Let us pay her a visit, shall we?"

Mrs Browner was not at her desk but there was an advent calendar lying open on top of it. Someone had scribbled something in the margin. Mr Holmes looked at it more closely. "Caught in the act," he said, sounding pleased.

The inspector glanced at the calendar sceptically. "Holmes, if you ask me, you are seeing things. That is just a list of ingredients for a bumper British breakfast. You should see the notes I scribble in my notebook during all the long and tedious phone calls I have to make. I have played whole tournaments of noughts and crosses against Mr Gregson – and I will have you know, I beat him every time."

"Congratulations," Holmes said. "But I can assure you you are not going to catch Moriarty this time either. He knows exactly where you intend to spring your trap on him! A famous London landmark, or so I believe."

shake them!

2, 6, 7

1, 5

1, 4

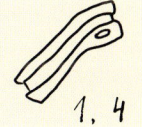

7, 8, 10

4, 5

A MOLE IN THE WORKS Solution

"Unless I'm very much mistaken, you are expecting Moriarty to show up at the Globe Theatre, am I right? The theatre is a huge tourist attraction and it will be easy to position a whole horde of plain-clothes police officers there."

Inspector Lestrade could not hide his surprise. "Holmes, you're a sly old fox! How do you know? You must tell me!"

"With the help of those doodles of course. The ones you mistakenly assumed were a list of ingredients. The drawings are part of a masked message. Let me show you how to decipher it. We have a list of food: sausages, toast, bacon, scrambled eggs and mushrooms. The numbers beneath the drawings tell us which letters to take. If we put those together, we are left with AGETTBOLEEHR and a clue we are meant to take literally: shake them! By placing the letters in the correct order, we end up with GLOBE THEATRE. That must surely mean the present-day replica of the original theatre built in 1599.

So we have found the mole - but she must have got suspicious when she saw me arrive. She has done a runner, I am afraid. Her boss has managed to pull his head out of the noose yet again. I wouldn't have too many high hopes about catching Moriarty, if I were you, considering the tools at your disposal. He will manage to get away. Believe me, I am speaking from experience."

Roasts Most Ruined

"How ridiculous!" Watson exclaimed, looking up from the newspaper article, which had caught his attention. Beside him, Holmes was snoozing in front of the blazing fire. "The lengths people will go to for the sake of a prize-winning Christmas roast turkey. Listen to this, Holmes."

LONDON'S CHRISTMAS ROAST SCANDAL

Pandemonium at this year's competition for the best roast turkey in all of London. Security was at an all-time high. The contestants were not even allowed to leave their workspaces to visit the toilet unless they were accompanied. They couldn't bring their own ingredients either. The exact quantities were provided according to their specifications. The large competition kitchen was divided into four separate cooking areas, each fully equipped with its own cooker and refrigerator as well as all the necessary utensils. However, when the four finalists finally presented their roasts to the jury several hours later, the judges were shocked. One roast after another turned out to be inedible. They didn't even try the first one, because it was burnt to a cinder, having been cooked at too high a temperature. There was no sign of a technical failure. The second turkey actually had stones in the stuffing! The filling of the third was delicious but the bird had been rubbed with sugar instead of salt. Only the fourth entry was impeccable. All hell broke loose, when candidate number four was declared the winner – for the fifth time in a row. The other candidates immediately accused her of cheating. They were convinced their roasts had been sabotaged by the winning candidate. In fact, it did seem unlikely that all the other candidates – who had successfully cooked their way into the finals – should have made such terrible mistakes. The jury has retired to decide whether the winner should be disqualified. There is something fishy going on. But can the jury prove it?

Roasts Most Ruined

"You're right, Watson," said Holmes as he filled his pipe. "It sounds very far-fetched." Watson folded up the newspaper: "The woman didn't need to do that, considering she has already won the competition four times in a row."

"Exactly! I am certain she did no wrong, but there is definitely a conspiracy going on. Of course, it's not entirely impossible that the oven for roast number one might have been turned up too high to start with, with all the hectic going on. But the roast remained in the oven for several hours and needed to be basted regularly. Did that particular candidate not notice that their roast was burning? Roast number three was rubbed with sugar instead of salt - perhaps the culprit swapped the ingredients, but where did that sugar come from? The candidates had to hand in their ingredient lists. All the items were purchased for them and they received the exact amounts they had asked for. Anyone who ordered sugar would have found it in their cooking area, ready and waiting. Moreover, the stuffing was perfect, so the sugar and salt didn't get mixed up. It is especially odd that roast number two's stuffing was full of stones: None of the candidates could leave their workplaces without a supervisor - and yet we are expected to believe the winner crept over to one of her rival's turkeys and added the stones to the stuffing mixture without being seen. And how come no one noticed those stones while they were stuffing the bird? I am certain the three other candidates joined forces to set the defending champion up. They deliberately ruined their own roasts in order to discredit the person who won."

Mad as a Hatter

Sippwick Hatters was printed in crooked letters on the workshop window. Through the glass, Watson and Holmes, who had chanced upon the place during their stroll, could see an elderly woman in a leather apron dashing this way and that. At her feet, a young woman also clad in an apron lay on the floor.

When Holmes knocked, the elderly woman opened the door. "Mishress Sippwick, the milliner, what canna do forru?" She asked gruffly. She was holding a roll of felt under her arm. The detective pointed to the woman on the ground. "Is your assistant feeling all right?" – "Unforshunately not!" – "Have you called the doctor?" – "No time!" – "Well, it's a lucky coincidence that I happen to have one with me, then!" – They pushed their way past the old woman. The person lying on the floor was deathly pale and there was no sign of a pulse. She lay between the remnants of a broken bowl and white powder and going by her temperature, she had been dead for several hours.

Watson said: "We won't be able to say if she died of natural causes until after the autopsy. Maybe her heart . . ."

In her bizarre way, the hat maker explained that the girl had simply keeled over and not got up again. "Lazyshing! After jush fourteen hours onnago!" She certainly had not gone to her aid, the hatter said. As far as she was concerned, the demise of the girl who had only started working for her in the run-up to Christmas, was a terrible inconvenience. "No one goes-ome whenneywant," she told the two baffled men. "Sippwick hatssarin such great demand this time ayear." She went on to say that every self-respecting Father Christmas impersonator in London commissioned their pointed hats at her workshop where they were manufactured in the traditional way.

"We must inform the police and contact her relatives at once," Holmes said. "What was the name of the deceased?"

"Um . . ." The hat maker stared into the air bleakly. Watson noticed her hands were shaking. "She's very agitated – something is terribly wrong," he whispered to his friend. "Do you think she poisoned her assistant?"

"Poisoning is to blame, but it is not what you are thinking," Holmes replied.

"This substance," Holmes pointed at the broken bowl and white powder strewn on the floor, "It's mercuric nitrate is it not?" The hat maker nodded. "We ushit to produce the felt forrerrats."

"You must surely be aware that the technique is very outdated?"

"Weesa tradishional business."

Watson interrupted them: "Mercury poisoning. Of course!" he cried. "Anyone coming into close contact with mercury for any length of time can become seriously ill! It gradually damages liver and kidneys and eventually the brain. Side effects include uncontrollable shaking, a detachment from reality and the inability to remember or articulate things clearly. One becomes . . ."

"As mad as a hatter!" Holmes finished the sentence for him. "That is where the old saying comes from. The real victim of poisoning here is Mistress Sippwick. The hired help's demise is an unfortunate side effect. In her delirium, the hat maker forced the poor girl to work more and more, without any breaks, day in day out. Her health was so seriously affected she ended up dying of exhaustion. The Japanese have a word for that: Karōshi - death by overwork."

"A workashident," the hat maker cried.

"One waiting to happen! And as you weren't even daunted by the prospect of working alongside a corpse, I doubt we can expect you to see reason. Those Father Christmasses are going to have to order their hats from the second-best hat maker in town, because you, Mistress Sippwick, need to go to hospital immediately. It will be for the doctors to decide whether or not you will be called to answer for working your employees to the bone . . ."

"This is a truly horrendous story." said **Dr Watson** as he and **Mr Holmes** reread the letter that had arrived that morning:

Dear Mr Holmes,

My name is James O'Connor and I am writing to you directly from prison. I am in custody, suspected of murdering my first wife. Things do not look good for me, but I protest my innocence. You are my last hope. Allow me to tell you about the case: I am accused of having poisoned my former wife with arsenic on the first of December. I am the main suspect, since I was the last person to be seen with her before she died. I wanted to make her a peace offering when we met that day. I had just come back from a three-week honeymoon with my new wife and the Season of Goodwill was upon us. Since our divorce a year ago, my ex-wife had made my life misery. I wanted to appeal to her conscience one last time before I would have to press charges against her. She did not look well. I know all about her serious illness, which could have been fatal, but which she had conquered a few years back. However, on that day, it seemed to me that the sickness had returned. My ex-wife was pale, weak, and had problems concentrating. Her skin was bad: There were grey spots on her face, and when I glanced at her ankles, they seemed to be almost black. In addition, she must have been working very hard of late. I am afraid I cannot pay her very much maintenance. Her hands were raw and badly callused. It breaks my heart to see her life end like this. However, if I am to blame for her death, it is because of the grief I caused her, and the relapse of her illness, not because I poisoned her. I truly believe the illness killed her. She often used arsenic to poison the rats. Maybe she inhaled some of that accidently and the coroner thought she must have been poisoned. Please help me, Mr Holmes!

Yours, James O'Connor

The Season of Good Will Solution

"Arsenic poisoning does seem to be a possibility," said Dr Watson, as he lent over the letter. "I can, however, rule out an accident with rat poison. She would have had to inhale a terrific amount to do herself any harm. Nonetheless, the symptoms concur with arsenic poisoning. The calloused hands and grey blotchy skin are known as arsenical melanosis. She even seems to have had black foot disease, damaged blood vessels caused by arsenic poisoning. Why would Mr O'Connor describe these symptoms in his letter if he had caused them by poisoning her?"

"Of course it could be malicious intent, but you are missing an essential detail, Watson," Mr Holmes said. "I too suspect arsenic poisoning. However, we need to differentiate: Mr O'Connor is accused of acutely poisoning his wife on the 1st of December, yet the symptoms his ex-wife demonstrated on that fateful day are the signs of chronic poisoning. The coroner in charge of the case must be a greenhorn. Muscle atrophy, anaemia, blotchy skin, dying blood vessels, all indicate the consumption of small amounts of arsenic over a long period of time. Symptoms of acute arsenic poisoning include violent vomiting, seizures, etc. Yet how could he have administered arsenic to his ex-wife on a regular basis while he was on his honeymoon? It seems more likely to me that this woman, impoverished, abandoned as she was, hated her ex-husband's newfound happiness and sought one last terrible revenge. Mr O'Connor mentioned a serious illness - perhaps it had returned and was proving to be fatal. Doomed to die, I believe she sought revenge against the man who had brought her nothing but sorrow, and made it look as if he had killed her. Of course, this is still just a theory. We must have it checked. But if it turns out I'm right, I will do everything in my power to make sure Mr O' Connor is home by Christmas."

The Abominable Snowman at Trafalgar Square

Shouts of surprise rang out around Trafalgar Square where people had flocked to see the magnificent Christmas tree standing almost 80-feet tall: "Look! Over there!" – "My goodness!" – "What the devil is it?" Christmas shoppers laden with bags of presents stopped in their tracks and craned their necks to see what was happening. In no time at all a crowd had gathered. Holmes, who was on his way back from the scene of a robbery in a nearby exclusive boutique, pushed his way through the gathering until he could go no further. Holmes tugged the trouser leg of a man who had climbed up a lamppost to get a better view. "What's going on?"

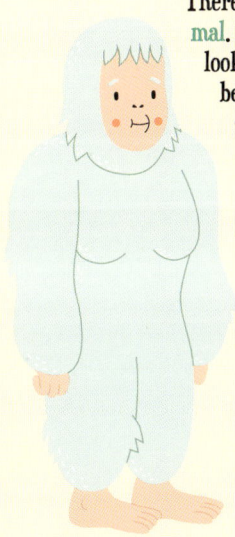

"There are loads of coppers over there," the man shouted. "They have cornered a wild animal. Now . . ." – "A wild animal? In the middle of London? What does it look like?" – "It looks almost human, but is covered in hair. It's . . . it's an abominable snowman!" – "Don't be ridiculous, let me take a look!"

The man climbed down and Holmes took his place. Over the heads of the crowd, he could see a scuffle going on. Four police officers whose tall helmets had been knocked crooked on their heads had surrounded the hairy monster. They took it in turns to throw themselves on the back of the beast but were flung off again immediately. The being was a grotesque mixture of different animals: Like a dancing bear, it swayed on two legs, its broad back covered in brown bristles. The beast had furry grey arms and a stomach coated in yellow fur with black spots. A pair of floppy thin legs dangled in front of its brown paws and small bits of paper stuck to different parts of its body. "Just as I thought," Holmes said. "It may be behaving wildly, but it is not the Abominable Snowman."

Some of the people standing close by looked up to him clinging to the lamppost. "What is it then?" – "What kind of animal?"

"A common furrere furem."

"A what?"

The Abominable Snowman at Trafalgar Square

"Furrure furem - that's Latin," Holmes told his audience. "Though criminalists like myself might also use the word 'fur-thief'."

"Is it human?"

"Certainly not one who cares about law and order. As luck would have it, I have just come from an exclusive clothes shop where there was a robbery today. Of course, they had stocked a variety of furs for the winter - coats, hats and shawls. Our robber stole more than he could carry unnoticed. I deduce he attempted to disguise himself with the stolen goods as he fled."

"What makes you think so?"

"All the different furs. He is wearing the skin of a brown bear over his head and back, a jaguar skin around his chest and stomach and in his hands, he is holding something that looks a lot like . . . yes, it's chinchilla. Those are all exceptionally expensive types of fur. The thief seems to have gone by the price tags - which he has had no time to remove and which I can see quite clearly from here."

"What a load of humbug!" someone in the group shouted.

"Not at all. Look - they have relieved him of the bearskin at last. And what do we see? Not the Abominable Snowman, just an unkempt London thief of the type one might find a hundredfold in the cheapest bars of the city, busy planning another robbery tour. Ladies and gentlemen, you will have to wait until Christmas to see a real marvel, I am afraid."

Oh, Christmas Tree

Would you prefer a Nordmann Fir or a Norway Spruce, Holmes?" Dr Watson asked, expertly examining two six-foot trees in front of him. However, before Holmes could demonstrate his lack of interest with a shrug, a Christmas Tree salesman hurried over. He looked as white as a sheet. "Gentlemen, we've got nothing to sell. Get your hands off my trees!" Shocked, Watson let go of the ones he had been looking at. "But I was just ..." - "I'm sorry sir, you don't understand. Those trees are riddled with vermin. Bark beetles! I can't think why. I know all the signs of bark beetle infestation and I always check the trees very carefully before I commit to a purchase. I must have overlooked something. See?" He pointed to the ground at the bottom of the trees, which was covered in a thin layer of sawdust. "That's the first sign. I have looked under the bark of several trees and there is no doubt about it. I don't know what I'm going to do." He wiped away the sweat from his brow. "This will be the ruin of me. A total and utter disaster. I usually live off the money I earn selling Christmas trees in the run-up to Christmas for the rest of the year." Dr Watson and Mr Holmes exchanged surprised glances. "I'm awfully sorry," Watson said, furtively wiping his hands on a handkerchief.

"What's that you are holding?" Holmes asked suddenly. The salesman stared at the white piece of paper between his fingers, as if he had forgotten it was there. "Oh that? It was stuck under the door of my stall this morning." He showed it to the two men.

> With best wishes to Lester Raye & Mirella Tickle.
> Yours, Anna Gramm

"I have no idea what it's about. My name is Wood and my assistant's name is Spruce. I don't know anyone called Anna Gramm." - "Anna Gramm, indeed." Holmes muttered. "I can't help you with the pest infestation. But I can give you a significant clue as to who might be behind this."

Oh, Christmas Tree Solution

"The message here isn't from someone called 'Anna Gramm'. It is an anagram in itself – the words are formed by rearranging the letters of another word. Lester Raye comes from 'tree slayer'. And Mirella Tickle is 'climate killer'."

"Holy smoke . . ." groaned Mr Wood, ruffling his hair. "I've got a hunch who this is."

"It's no coincidence that this note turned up out of the blue on the very same day you noticed the pest infestation," Mr Holmes said. "It's likely that local environmentalists and tree lovers wanted to teach you a lesson. I suspect those beetles were, shall we say, 'relocated' to these trees shortly after you purchased them, in order to destroy your merchandise. The perpetrators waited the time it took for the infestation to become apparent before sending you this cryptic message."

The Christmas tree salesman grabbed Holmes' hands and addressed him with tears in his eyes. "Mr Holmes, thank you ever so much! I would never have guessed what this message was all about, but now I have a good idea who did this to me. There were some altercations earlier this year with two certain people . . . If I get myself a good lawyer, I might be able to claim damages and be saved from ruin."

Holmes wished him well and let Dr Watson lead the way to another Christmas tree stand.

The Little Mistress

Holmes entered one of the sparsely furnished interrogation rooms at Scotland Yard after scraping at least a pound of dripping slush from his shoes. Slush that had lost any similarity to nice fresh snow - as he repeatedly told the porter.

"Confess, Mrs Simpson!" Inspector Lestrade shouted at a young woman. "You've got to confess!"

"Lestrade, why in heavens name did you ask me to come here? And quieten down please, the noise is unbearable!" - "Forgive me, Holmes. You are right of course. But I've almost solved this case: We were called to a property by a neighbour reporting an escalating row between a married couple. We found this woman's husband in the gazebo in the grounds of his estate." - "And what does her husband have to say on the matter?" - "Nothing much, Holmes. Nothing at all in fact. He's dead. Stabbed 24 times. With a fillet knife. It was in the knife block, as innocent as can be, all shiny and clean. But the tiniest tip of the point was missing which we found about an hour ago in one of the victim's ribs." - "And then what?" - "The couple were famous for their rows all over the neighborhood. It wasn't the first time we were called to their property." - "I'm sorry, Lestrade. I simply don't understand why you have asked me to attend."

"Mrs Ophelia Janet Simpson - that's her full name - denies everything."

"Mrs Simpson, would you please recount the course of events as you recall them?"

"Certainly, sir. We had argued, of course. It happens all the time. My husband has a lover you see. I wouldn't be the least bit surprised if she was behind this. When I found my husband, I saw someone hurrying away across the road. A very petite woman."

"Here Holmes. We found this fine leather glove in the gutter, covered in Mr Simpson's blood. We have had it analysed. All the evidence confirms that the murderer wore it. The problem is, it can't have been Mrs Simpson after all, because the glove is far too small!"

"Oh Lestrade . . ."

The Little Mistress

"My dear Inspector, you might be in the service of her Majesty the Queen, but you have missed an important detail. What are the roads like right now, in the middle of winter - the ground, the tarmac the cobbled streets - do we have black ice or snow?"

"No. Slush. The snow from the past few days has turned to a sludgy mess. It's horrendous."

"Precisely. Soaking wet dirty slush. And the glove was found in the gutter full of blood! It must have been dripping wet."

"It was indeed - when we found it. It's only slightly damp now."

"Then it's no wonder Mrs Simpson's hand is far too big to fit even remotely. Wet leather shrinks significantly as it dries. It is a similar effect to washing a woollen jumper in hot water. Knowing this, Mrs Simpson deliberately threw the glove into the soaking gutter along the route the culprit was supposed to have taken. Unfortunately for her, you have already proved that no suspect with little hands could have fled, taking the murder weapon with her - because the tip of the knife in the house was found in the victim's body. Mrs Simpson, I think you will find the rigged murder scene will not stand up to any proper scrutiny.

The manufacturer of this stylish glove should not be too difficult to find. Ask him to determine its original size, Lestrade, and then get your suspect to try on one that size. I bet you will find it's a perfect fit."

Daylight Robbery 15

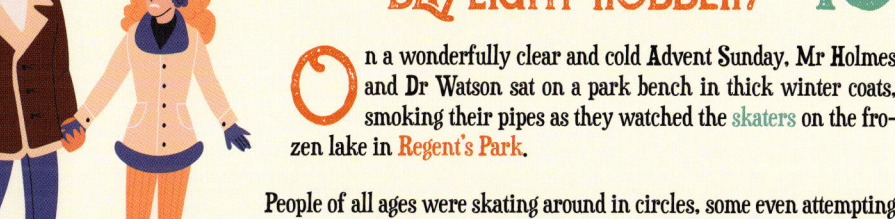

On a wonderfully clear and cold Advent Sunday, Mr Holmes and Dr Watson sat on a park bench in thick winter coats, smoking their pipes as they watched the skaters on the frozen lake in Regent's Park.

People of all ages were skating around in circles, some even attempting the odd pirouette or two while children pulled their friends across the ice on sledges. An elderly gentleman was busy shovelling away snow and ice scraped up by the sharp blades. The winter sun sparkled on the dark shiny surface. Unfortunately, a ruffian was disturbing the peaceful scene by racing across the lake far too fast and bumping into the other skaters. People hollered loudly as he passed. Then suddenly someone shouted: "Stop! Stop thief! You won't get away with this!" A rather large lady, her face twisted in fury, chased after the rowdy at a surprising speed considering her size. One by one the other skaters checked their bags and pockets and then joined the chase, following the woman. Almost all of them were missing something.

The angry mob led by the large lady soon cornered the lout and crowded around him. Instead of calling the police, they searched him on the spot without any further ado. "I didn't do anything. I don't have your things! Leave me alone, are you crazy or something. I'll call the cops," the young man shouted. They found nothing and finally let go of him. "He hasn't got anything. He must be innocent." - "But it can't be a coincidence, him bumping into everyone and then our valuables gone missing!" - "Come on. Own up! Where are the stolen goods?"

Mr Holmes joined the circle of people. "Excuse me; I think I can be of assistance here."

DAYLIGHT ROBBERY SOLUTION

"Well I never, it's Sherlock Holmes! Please help us, Mr Holmes – he's robbed us all!" Mr Holmes smiled. "He certainly did. But you can search him all you like, he hasn't got the loot." – "Who's got it then? He never left the ice for a minute!"

"This lad has an accomplice who has just sneaked away. Do not worry, I have sent my dear friend Dr Watson after him. We will soon hear where he has hidden the pickings. Surely you noticed the elderly man diligently shoveling away the ice and snow to keep the surface smooth and clean? How very generous of him to provide a nice flat skating area for the general public. Especially at his age. However, he was not selfless after all. He was richly rewarded for his efforts. His partner in crime who you have managed to capture – perhaps you would like to loosen your grip dear lady, he's turning a little blue in the face – his partner, as you rightly assumed, relieved you of your belongings. But they did not disappear into his pockets. Instead, he dropped them on the ground where the old fellow scooped them up as fast as lightning and then thrust them under the reeds at the edge of the lake. As soon as the commotion started here, he gathered up the stolen goods and skedaddled. But not to worry, we are hot on his tail."

CLEAR-CUT CRIME

Like a heavy shower, shards of glass rained down on the customers in the fashionable boutique. Luckily, no one was injured by broken pieces of glass or by the person who plummeted to the ground. He hit the floor with such a force that the Christmas decorations on the shelves packed with shirts and blouses wobbled.

Holmes, who happened to be in the changing rooms trying on a dinner suit, charged out in sock soles and trousers that were too big for him. Unfortunately, the master glazier had not survived the fall. He and his apprentice had been replacing a cracked panel of glass in the transparent walkway on the first floor, which looked down on the salesroom twenty feet below.

A doctor was called to examine the dead body. Holmes headed up to the first floor where he found the panel of glass with a fine crack running through it next to the hole in the floor through which the glazier had fallen. The apprentice was crouched beside the hole, staring down at the scene below incredulously. Holmes questioned him immediately and the young man explained how he and his master had removed the broken panel of glass and carefully inserted a new one as they had done numerous times before. After they had puttied the panel, the master glazier trod on it with his full weight to make sure it had fitted into place properly, and it had simply given way beneath him. It was like falling through a trap door.

Holmes went back downstairs where two medics were about to take the dead man away. The caretaker was ready and waiting with his brush and dustpan. "One moment, please!" the detective said, stopping the men. "There is one more thing I'd like to check."

He picked up a splinter of glass from the ground and turned it this way and that between his fingers. Before anyone could stop him, he jammed it into the back of his hand. However, no blood squirted out. Then he popped it into his mouth, chewed it for a moment and finally spat out several smaller pieces. Amongst the crowd of onlookers, a woman fainted. Holmes turned to one of the shop employees. "Lock all the doors immediately. Let no one in or out except for the police - or else the culprit will get away!"

"This is outrageous!" the apprentice shouted as a police officer handcuffed him and brought him over to see the detective. "I'm innocent!"

"The manner in which you propelled your master into the life hereafter is what is truly outrageous," Holmes replied.

"We were only here to replace a glass panel ..." the young man shouted back, trying to free his bound hands.

"And so you did, but your master had no idea that you had swapped the new panel of normal glass for one made of sugar glass beforehand. It is used in the movies: For example, when someone is hurled through a barroom window, it will be made of sugar glass. Sugar glass consists of water and sugar which crystalises when it is boiled, forming a hard and transparent layer surprisingly similar to real glass. With your knowledge and skills, it was easy for you to make it. Sugar glass breaks easily – so transporting it would have been the most difficult part of your plan. You knew that the master always checked the quality of his work with his full body weight. Once you had fitted the panel, you could be sure that he would be the first to stand on it. When he did so, the sugar glass gave way as intended. A half-baked murder plot, seeing as the broken pieces of glass have no sharp edges. Even the most untalented police officers would have spotted that at once. Now they can concentrate on finding the motive for this malicious murder instead. Because I have to see if this suit is available in a smaller size."

Jesus and Mary

The elderly pensioner Mary Biggins had sent for Mr Holmes on a delicate matter. In the mood for an outing, Watson accompanied his friend to the London suburb of Whyteleafe. Mrs Biggins' sprawling house was crammed full of old furniture and trinkets, which Holmes regarded with disdain. Over tea, he asked the lady to explain her problem.

"I have a terrible feeling that my son John, who is my sole heir, wants the house for himself! Every time he comes to visit me – he has been here three times in the recent past, after not visiting me for years – he asks me if I would not feel more comfortable in a nursing home. At first, I thought nothing of it, but he has become so brash in the meantime, it is positively disconcerting. I wonder if he wants to sell the house because he has money problems. I can't imagine him wanting to live in it himself. What would he do with such a big house? After all, he has been single for years, and he is a townie through and through. He restores furniture and spends most of his time in his workshop anyway!"

"I'm very sorry, but I don't see how we can help," said Mr Holmes, visibly disappointed that there wasn't an exciting case waiting for him. "I can only advise you to live life as you please." With a polite farewell, he turned to leave.

On his way out, Watson noticed a mural hanging in the entrance hall. "Holmes! Look at this! Do you recall the incident at the Christmas fair in the British Museum only a few days ago? A false alarm went off because of the original of that painting!"

"Jesus in the Manger!" said Mrs Biggins. "I bought that copy more than fifty years ago at a local jumble sale and always put it up at Christmas. I fetched it from the attic only yesterday."

Mr Holmes' eyes lit up. "Once again, I'm delighted I brought you along, Watson. You have just discovered a detail that will be crucial in solving Mrs Biggins' problem."

"Congratulations, Mrs Biggins, what an exquisite find you made at that jumble sale all those years ago. If I am not mistaken, this is no cheap replica, but a centuries-old artefact worth thousands of pounds. Have you really been using this picture as a Christmas decoration for decades?

Your son is a restorer, as you told us – perhaps he even works regularly for the British Museum and had access to the exhibition where the false alarm was reported? Let us assume he does have money problems after all. Imagine his surprise when he discovers the picture of Jesus in the Manger in the exhibition – the original of the copy he knows from home. He soon developed a plan to swap the original and the copy. He visited you for the first time recently to make sure you still owned your painting, Mrs Biggins.

On his second visit, he removed it from the house. John Biggins must have known there would be a precarious moment when he swapped the two pictures, as the alarm would go off when he touched the original. Being a restorer, he could probably have talked his way out of trouble if he got spotted, but he was gone by the time the security guards arrived. On his third visit to you, he carried the original painting up to your attic so that you would not suspect anything when you went to fetch it.

The other potential flaw in his plan was that someone might notice the replica at the British Museum any moment. It speaks for his skill that he has managed to fool the experts and you so far. Eventually, however, he would have to sell the painting on the black market in order not to run the risk of the original being found here. You have become a thorn in his side because you are attached to the picture and would obviously notice if it disappeared. That is the reason for trying to drive you out of the house.

Let's get to the bottom of this right away by paying a visit to the British Museum and taking a closer look at the supposed original. Since you are fond of broadening your mind, I'm sure you won't object, Watson?"

False Charity

S pirits were high at the Gentlemen's Club. It was time to cele-brate the great success of this year's Christmas appeal for the London orphanages. "Five thousand and seventy-two pounds have landed in our collection box, gentlemen!" As Mr Richardson, the initiator of the appeal, held up the box full of all the pound notes, laughing, Holmes returned to the buffet.

"Good evening, Mr Holmes. You have not been around much lately, but obviously, you would not want to miss the Charity dinner. The sturgeon is excellent and goes very well with the Champagne," an elderly gentleman wearing tails addressed him. "Indeed," Mr Holmes agreed as he helped himself to some saddle of venison.

Behind them, Mr Richardson was tirelessly lauding the generosity of all the attending property magnates and barons. He pulled one bank note after the other out of the box to show to the listeners. "Just look at all these bank notes! Here is one with Churchill's image on it, the never-tiring defeater of fascism. Or perhaps you prefer Jane Austen, the genius who penned Pride and Prejudice, two character traits that are alien to all of us here, of course. This one shows William Wilberforce, who fought tirelessly to end slavery – what could be more charitable than that? In addition, here we have Adam Smith who demanded prosperity for all, no matter their birth or education . . ."

Mr Holmes set down his plate and turned around to Mr Richardson. The elderly gentleman asked him: "Is it not to your liking?" Instead of answering, the detective raised his voice: "I'm sorry to ruin the atmosphere for you all, but the result of your appeal isn't quite the figure you announced. There can be no talk of having five thousand and seventy-three pounds!"

Holmes' speech was followed by a deathly hush in the hall. Mr Richardson made a face similar to the sturgeon on the buffet. Then he croaked: "What are you saying, man?"

FALSE CHARITY Solution

"I'm saying there is forged money in that box."

There were harsh calls of protest. "One of us cheated?" – "Why on earth? To hurt the poor or to look good here?" – "How can you be so sure?"

Mr Holmes asked for quiet. "I'll explain in a minute. But first allow me to ask how much this magnificent buffet of the finest foods cost?"

Mr Richardson answered: "All in all, about six thousand pounds." – "An impressive sum! Six thousand pounds we could have donated to the orphanages. Instead, we prefer to consume it all. Tonight, we are celebrating no one but ourselves, gentlemen!"

There was another embarrassed silence. Holmes continued: "I doubt very much that a rich man was being stingy in this case, or that someone was trying to seem more generous than he could afford to be. The forger must have known he was going to be found out. Especially as everyone was expecting me to attend this event, as I do every year. No, this must be a wake-up call from an activist. He wanted to illustrate how we celebrate ourselves for no reason, while the true value of our donation lies way below the sum we are prepared to spend on ourselves on this occasion."

"He's trying to show us up!" Mr Richardson shouted angrily. "And he must still be in our midst!" He looked around the room angrily but the forger did not step forward.

Holmes answered: "Instead of trying to find the forger, why don't we remove the counterfeit money and pass around the collecting box again. The forger was kind enough to make the false notes clearly recognisable. There are notes with Churchill, Austen and Smith in circulation. However, William Wilberforce who fought against slavery never made it onto any bank note. Real fifty pound notes depict the inventors of the modern steam engine, James Watt and Matthew Boulton."

Looking embarrassed, the club members drew their wallets out of their pockets for the second time. None of them noticed that the elderly gentleman had left the club in the meantime . . .

A Ritual

It was just a few days before Christmas when Holmes opened the door to a totally fraught-looking police officer from the Yard and, on his bidding, immediately followed the man to Fletcher Street. In the spacious apartment of Lady Winterbottom, Inspector Gregson was waiting for Holmes, looking equally distraught.

"Holmes! London has never seen the like! Satanists, Holmes! Dark rites! Black masses! Human sacrifice! And just before Christmas! See for yourself. Heavens above! What is the world coming to?"

Holmes walked into the living room, which at first glance seemed very welcoming. The table was laden with baked gingerbread, German cinnamon star cookies and sugar-plum shortbread spread out on a number of pieces of greaseproof paper. The room was decorated with twigs and pine cones. There was a lovely smell of incense and pine needles, of candle wax and the greased paper, of ginger and butter and the fire burning in the tiled stove.

In the middle of the room, however, the body of an old woman lay sprawled across an impressive Persian rug. The corpse was anything but ordinary and it is just possible that for a moment a look of surprise crossed Holmes' usually impassive face.

"Look, Holmes. The woman is completely naked! Her clothes are strewn all over the place. And there are at least a dozen pentagrams slit into her skin. Pentagrams, Holmes! It's an unholy mess! The work of the devil. Secret brethren! Satanists! This is no ordinary murder! This is a ritual sacrifice! Crimes beyond the pale."

"Gregson, Gregson, Gregson. Satanic rites in old Lady Winterbottom's home? I am not so sure . . . Did you not notice the smell in the air? A bouquet of aromas, to be more precise? I can assure you there were no more Satanists here than you would expect to find at a service in Saint Paul's . . ."

A Ritual Solution

"Where to start? The wood in the stove, butter in the biscuit dough, ginger in the gingerbread, pine needles - they all go together to create a very specific scent. A familiar mixture we only ever experience in the run-up to Christmas. A singular and sensory experience, Gregson. Mrs Winterbottom had obviously been busy baking - three different kinds of biscuits in fact. She had put her creations out to cool on the large table. A third of those biscuits are cinnamon stars! Cinnamon stars! Cinnamon is a strong and very Christmassy spice and here we have one cinnamon star after the other, Gregson - can you smell cinnamon in this room? Cinnamon stars are usually full of the spice, but it seems to be totally missing here. Either Lady Winterbottom forgot to add any, or else she used something else by mistake. The question is: What did she use instead? Ground Cinnamon is a dark brown powder. Another brown powder commonly used in baking is nutmeg. Unfortunately, however, nutmeg can be lethal. It is only safe in very small doses. Just a pinch. But you need tablespoons of cinnamon. Now imagine Lady Winterbottom noticing her cinnamon biscuits tasting odd so she tries one after the other, wondering at the flavour.

Poor Lady Winterbottom - in her body, the spice quickly turned into such hideous substances as mescaline and amphetamine, causing the most severe hallucinations. In her frenzy, I believe she decided to make some more cinnamon stars. She removed her clothes and - insane as she was - tried to cut stars out of her body with the five-pointed cookie cutter. There you have your pentagrams! She continued her baking and cookie cutting - in a very hallucinogenic way.

Shortly thereafter, death must have occurred. Exitus. Cardiac arrest. Gregson - forensics will show whether my theory is correct. But just in case it is, hands off those cinnamon stars."

CHRISTMAS COOKIES

Mr Holmes and Dr Watson were enjoying two magnificent Honduran cigars with Watson's snoring bulldog lying at their feet when there was a tentative knock at the door. "Come in!" Watson called. To their astonishment, Mrs Hudson was at the door, looking embarrassed and hardly daring to step across the threshold. "Mrs Hudson, has something happened? Have I done anything wrong?" Holmes called in surprise. He had a quick think but could not remember doing anything to annoy his landlady over the past few days. He had not even played the violin in the middle of the night for a number of weeks.

"Um, not exactly," Mrs Hudson cleared her throat. "May I, um, may I ask for your help? I was just going to bake some Christmas cookies for the charity bazaar at the weekend when a wee problem cropped up." - "Christmas baking isn't exactly my forte, Mrs Hudson, you know." - "I don't want you to help me with the baking, just to read the recipe!" - "You are already wearing your glasses," Holmes said, puffing away at his cigar. Mrs Hudson thrust a piece of paper at him. "I coded the ingredient amounts last year and now I can't remember how to decode them again." Holmes glanced at her pensively. "Why would you write the recipe in code?" - "Well, because you poke your nose into everything in this house and I thought to myself, he's not getting my cookie recipes, that's my secret!"

Looking at her with something close to respect, Holmes tried with difficulty to suppress a laugh. "My dear Mrs Hudson, what would I want with your recipes? I cannot bake - I would never dream of doing such a thing. Still, no worries, we will soon sort this out . . ."

Flour (g)	545 — 533 — 512 — ? — 479
Butter (g)	4 — 9 — 45 — 50 — ?
Almonds (g)	40 — 44 — 52 — 68 — ?
Sugar (g)	5 — 10 — 100 — ? — 40.000
Eggs	720 — 120 — 24 — 6 — ?
1 tsp. baking powder	

CHRISTMAS COOKIES Solution

"You have chosen some rather simple number series, I see. Merely mildly challenging." Holmes held the piece of paper close to Mrs Hudson's eyes. "Stop keeping poor Mrs Hudson under suspense, Holmes," Dr Watson said. "You are a mean old tease."

Mr Holmes ignored him. "Look here: For flour, subtract 12 and 21 alternately: 545 minus 12 is 533, minus 21 is 512, minus 12 is 500, minus 21 is 479. With the butter, you have to add 5 and multiply by 5 in turn: 4 plus 5 is 9, times 5 is 45, plus 5 is 50, times 5 is 250. Let us move on to the almonds – here the value that is added is always doubled: 40 plus 4 is 44, plus 8 is 52, plus 16 is 68, plus 32 is 100. The sugar is slightly more complex. It has to be alternately multiplied by 2 and then squared: 5 times 2 is 10; 10 squared is 100;

times 2 is 200; 200 squared is 40,000. Now to the eggs and you can start baking immediately. Here you divide with the next smallest number: 720 divided by 6 is 120, divided by 5 is 24, divided by 4 is 6, divided by 3 is 2. Therefore, you need 500g of flour, 250g of butter, 100g of ground almonds, 200g of sugar, 2 eggs and a teaspoon of baking powder. Now for my reward. I am sure you won't mind giving me some of your lovely biscuits, will you?"

"Of course not, Mr Holmes," Mrs Hudson mumbled and disappeared with a bright red face.

An Explosive Solo

Watson. How kind of you to bring me to this shady jazz bar. But ... what can we expect to hear?" Holmes looked around with suspicion. Hardly any of the small tables were occupied. – "Free improvisation on the theme of popular Christmas carols, my dear friend. It will make a nice change." – "Ah."

A stagehand was busy carting in the instruments. He dropped the bass and guitar onto their stands and set up the drums in a few brisk routine movements, though he handled the bass drum with great care. The drum skin was probably rather delicate. As soon as he had finished, the three musicians appeared on stage. The stagehand greeted them each with a friendly kiss on the right cheek before he disappeared into the wings.

When the guitar player turned around to his colleagues to discuss their cues, Holmes spotted the tattoo of a knife on the back of his neck. The other musicians also had tattoos. The bass player had black spots tattooed on his knuckles and the drummer had gravestones on his arms.

"Do you think they can capture the Christmas spirit?" Watson said under his breath. The bass player began to play a succession of notes. As the guitar player joined in, the melody of Jingle Bells started to take shape. "Not bad." Watson whispered to Holmes. "Don't you agree?"

However, before Holmes could answer, the drummer joined in with a roll. As he stepped on the pedal and the beater touched the membrane of the bass drum, there was a huge explosion. The drummer and a large part of the stage disappeared. Bits of wood flew everywhere as Holmes and Watson were flung from their chairs.

Within just a few minutes, the police and fire brigade had arrived.

Holmes and Watson checked to make sure they weren't injured before they joined the helpers with their ears still ringing.

"What on earth happened?" the doctor panted.

"A bomb went off." Holmes answered. "and what's more – we were warned!"

"But why didn't you prevent it, if you knew it was going to happen?" Watson asked.

"I didn't understand the signs in time."

"Holmes, you must tell us what is going on! We were very nearly blown up. I want to know what happened here! Why was the band the target of a bomb attack?"

The two seriously injured musicians were carried off the stage past them on stretchers. Sadly, there wasn't much of the drummer left to attend to.

"These musicians are members of a criminal gang. You will have noticed the tattoos - signs of the Russian Mafia. The knife on the back of the neck is the sign of a hitman, the dots on the knuckles recount the number of years a person has been in prison and the same goes for the gravestones. Everyone on stage was a hardened criminal."

"And who was out to get them?"

"The stagehand. The kiss on the cheek is the kiss of death in the Sicilian mafia, the Cosa Nostra, which is battling the Russian Mafia for influence here in London. Whoever is given the kiss has been sentenced to death and has just a short time left to live. It seems that I wasn't the only one who missed the sign, the musicians did too. The way the killer handled that bass drum so carefully, I assume it was filled with a considerable amount of nitro glycerine. That is an unstable chemical, which releases extreme energy at the slightest jolt - and hey presto, it explodes!"

"We should inform the police at once." As they headed towards one of the police officers who were trying to sort out the chaos, the detective hummed a melody.

"Holmes, how can you!" Watson stared at him indignantly. "That's Jingle Bells you are humming."

"It certainly went off with a bang, didn't it?"

The body was lying curled up in the straw. It almost looked like it was sleeping, but there was no movement in the little chest. "He was still so young," Tommy exclaimed under tears, "we only got him a few weeks ago on St Nicholas day. I always wanted to have a dwarf hamster even though Tamara was against the idea because she doesn't agree with keeping animals in cages."

Mr Holmes examined Fred the dead dwarf hamster and gave Watson a reproachful look. As he checked the cage for leftover food and excrement, he discovered that the hamster suffered from severe diarrhea in its final hours. Watson had asked Holmes for a favour and then driven him to a friend whose hamster had died that morning. Now they were all standing around the cage: Mr and Mrs Turner, who ran their doctor's surgery in the home where they lived with their son Tommy and their elder daughter Tamara. In a cracked voice, Tamara had recounted finding the body. Now she was sad and silent while Tommy picked up the story.

"Only yesterday, Tamara and I collected titbits for him in the garden. I found some long yellow flowers that looked like tentacles on a bush and Tamara picked some flat white ones about this size." Tommy held up his finger and thumb indicating a length of about four inches. "He loved them."

Holmes stopped examining the hamster's cage. "Well that explains what caused this creature's unfortunate predicament," he said. "One of those flowers is not for eating - by humans or hamsters."

Watson interrupted him looking sceptical. "So you can tell from one short description which flowers we are talking about? Shouldn't we go out to the garden to be sure?"

Flower Power Solution

"My dear Watson, the short unscientific descriptions are all I need to explain this sudden death. How many plants do you know that grow in our region and flower in December when the days are at their shortest and the temperatures around zero? Not many, I am sure. No doubt, Mrs Turner will confirm that she has a Hamamelis in her garden, more commonly known as witch-hazel, a bush with yellow blossoms and a strong fragrance. They often flower in December as Tommy noticed yesterday. It poses no threat and was neither poisonous nor dangerous for dear little Fred. In fact, the very opposite is true. It is often used for medicinal purposes.

The Lenten rose, also known as the Christmas rose, is a very different matter. Surely it too can be found in Mrs Turner's garden. Tamara picked some of the flowers to feed the hamster. It is a popular ornamental plant, but is extraordinarily toxic to humans and animals due to a combination of cardiotoxic bufadienolides, ecdysones, saponins and protoanemonin. These substances caused the unfortunate rodent to suffer from severe diarrhea – just look at the cage if you want to sure – and obviously led to a circulatory collapse with subsequent organ failure.

Only one question remains: Was it an accident, Tamara? I suspect this is more than a sad coincidence."

Tamara burst out: "I felt so sorry for him!" she sobbed. "In his small, narrow cage – all alone – what kind of life did he have here? I just felt sorry for him."

"Tamara!" cried Mrs Turner. "You should have talked to us, instead of . . ."

"I don't want to judge," said Mr Holmes. "But don't forget that hamsters, unlike many other rodents, are solitary animals by nature, and it is quite possible to read up on what can be done to make their living conditions perfectly adequate, even in cages."

CHRISTMAS BAUBLES

Holmes, here you are at last!" Lestrade beckoned Mr Holmes into the Sainsbury family's living room, the scene of the crime. In the middle of the room stood a magnificently decorated Christmas tree, under which a pile of broken red Christmas baubles lay instead of presents. Next to the tree, two police officers were guarding a tied-up man. The Sainsbury family of four, dressed in their pyjamas and dressing gowns, stood huddled in the corner of the room looking very intimidated. "That's the burglar," Lestrade said, pointing to the man in handcuffs. "The family's burglar alarm went off and notified the police who were able to apprehend him. He is the chief suspect concerning a series of burglaries at five further homes. Broken red Christmas tree baubles were found at each of the six apartments. He won't tell us anything."

Holmes squatted down in front of the fine pieces of broken glass. "All of them were red?" He fished out one of the bauble hooks from among the shards. 'Harrods limited edition 89' was stamped on it in small letters. "A limited edition?" he asked the Sainsburys. "Err, yes," Mrs Sainsbury replied. "I bought the set of 10 for us in early December. A designer edition made exclusively for Harrods and limited to 100 baubles." - "Did you notice anything strange about these baubles?" - "Apart from being so absolutely gorgeous? No. Although wait, one of the baubles was unusually heavy. Far heavier than the others. We didn't hang it up because the Christmas tree branches bent so much under its weight and it threatened to fall off."

Holmes stood up and pointed at the captured man. "Have you been able to find out anything about this man, Lestrade?" - "I have indeed. He was in custody for a few days only recently. There was a scuffle between him and a former colleague who had accused him of stealing. They let him go when they couldn't prove anything." - "Who was his employer?" - "Harrods. He was a sales clerk there. Is that a good reason to break into innocent families' homes and destroy their Christmas baubles?"

CHRISTMAS BAUBLES SOLUTION

"This case reminds me of another one in my long career," Holmes said. "Can you bring me the heavy Christmas tree bauble please, Mrs Sainsbury?" She left the room and returned with another red bauble. Holmes took it from her and gently pulled on the hook. "It's a tight fit." At the same moment, he dropped the bauble and it shattered on the parquet floor. The shouts of protest from the Sainsburys died away as Holmes lifted a delicate diamond bracelet out of the debris.

"This confirms my suspicions. This is a stolen piece of jewellery, which our burglar probably hid in one of the baubles during his time at Harrods. If you undo the hook at the top, you can easily slide a bracelet into the hollow sphere. And look! It has the Harrods stamp on it. I imagine our burglar was caught stealing the bracelet by his colleague with whom he clashed and who called the police. The thief managed to hide the bracelet before the police arrived. Unfortunately for him, he was taken into custody and had no idea what happened to that bauble. Fortunately, it was one of a special edition limited to ten packs which were rather expensive and therefore not paid for in cash. Thus, all our burglar had to do was to get hold of the names of account holders who had ordered the baubles and then find out where they lived. So this will not be his sixth, but in fact his seventh burglary in search of his lost bauble. As a former employee, he obviously knew how to get into Harrods and find the data. We will have to look into that. As soon as he had the addresses, he broke the red designer balls in one household after the other in order to recover the stolen goods. Did I mention that I once had a similar case concerning six busts of Napoleon? Perhaps you remember, Lestrade. If not, my faithful friend Watson is sure to have written about it, so you can read it at your leisure."

Freezing fog had shrouded the city of London in a frosty powder of glistening white. Over the last hour, the winter dusk had blanketed the dim light coming from the streetlamps and windows. Christmas Eve gave the city an unreal aura. The streets and pavements, shops and parks were empty - every part of this vibrant, buzzing city seemed to have come to a halt.

Even Holmes could not resist the all-encompassing sense of inertia. As on every Christmas Eve, he was spending the evening with his brother Mycroft in the Diogenes Club not far from the Carlton Hotel on Pall Mall.

"Sherly, my dear! You actually managed to impress me this year. How did you solve the case of the giant rat of Sumatra - what were the circumstances?" - "Mycroft, let's leave it to dear Watson to recount my cases, shall we?" - "Just as you wish, Sherly. How is the good Doctor? It must be over a year since I last set eyes on him ..." - "You won't believe it, Mycroft, but under the influence of shortbread and punch he has devised a plan to present my more complex cases in a regular crime column. It is to be published in the Strand Magazine next December. Day by day for twenty four days, we hope to entertain the readers in the run-up to Christmas." - "What a ridiculous idea." - "I quite agree." - "Let's not forget our own tradition, our Christmas charade, with all this talking. It is more difficult this time, Sherly - a single riddle with no questions allowed and just the one answer. Are you ready?" - "Ready when you are, Mycroft. Of course!"

"Right then:

It is a gift of old
Its first is forthright and bold
Its second to anger and provoke
It fills the air with strong fragrant smoke."

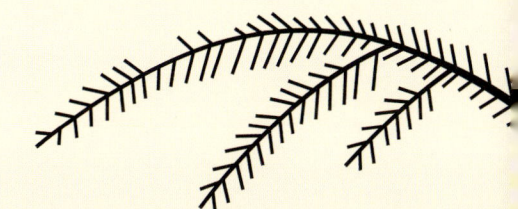

A Charade Solution

"Mycroft, once again you disappoint me, like you do every year. This riddle is far too easy for me!"

"Then let's hear the answer!"

"You are looking for a compound noun. The first word is forthright and bold: frank is the answer! Now for the second word: to anger and provoke. It must be incense. A gift of old that fills the air with a strong fragrant smoke - noble or holy smoke, I presume. Certainly not the blue haze of your cigars or my pipe tobacco. The solution, my dear brother, is frankincense, a gift of the Magi! Oh, you really are a sentimental old so and so. You pretend to despise Christmas and then ask me this riddle on Christmas Eve!"

"Just once a year, perhaps, I do allow myself a little sentimentality. It keeps me sane the rest of the time, dear Sherly. Which is more than can be said for you."

"Well, if that is so, I will join in and make that sacrifice, too - in support of a sane mind. So, Merry Christmas, dear Mycroft. Merry Christmas and a Happy New Year!"

"And you, too, dear Sherly. You and all those pitiful readers of Watson's absurd scribblings. Merry Christmas and a Happy New Year!"